For Ivan and Giacomo
D.C.

For Ann'so
S.M.

Little Pea's Drawing School
Text copyright © 2021 by Davide Cali
Illustration copyright © 2021 by Sébastien Mourrain
First edition copyright © 2021 Comme des géants

All rights reserved.

Editorial and art direction by Nadine Robert
Translation by Nick Frost
Book design by Jolin Masson

The illustrations in this book were made with ink and digitally colored.
This book was typeset in Louize.

This edition published in 2022 by Milky Way Picture Books,
an imprint of Comme des géants inc. Varennes, Quebec, Canada.

Library and Archives Canada Cataloguing in Publication

Title: Little Pea's drawing school / Davide Calì;
illustrations, Sébastien Mourrain; translation, Nick Frost.
Other titles: École de dessin de Petit Pois. English
Names: Calì, Davide, 1972– author. | Mourrain, Sébastien, 1976– illustrator. |
Frost, Nick, translator.
Description: Translation of: L'école de dessin de Petit Pois.
Identifiers: Canadiana 20210066873 | ISBN 9781990252075 (hardcover)
Classification: LCC PZ7.1.C35 Li 2022 | DDC j843/.92—dc23

ISBN 978-1-990252-07-5

Printed and bound in China

Milky Way Picture Books
38 Sainte-Anne Street
Varennes, QC J3X 1R5
Canada

www.milkywaypicturebooks.com

story by
Davide Cali

art by
Sébastien Mourrain

Little
Pea's
Drawing School

Milky Way
Picture Books

Do you know Little Pea?
He's a great artist.
Everyone loves him!
This is his home studio,
where he spends his days working away.

In his career, Little Pea's specialty
has been drawing stamp collections.

There's this one on flowers.

This one on insects
created a real buzz.

And another on mountains.

And, naturally,
he made one on trees.

Young artists often come
to him for advice and encouragement.
"Hmmm… how interesting!" he'll say.

"Little Pea, you should open an art
school for drawing," a friend suggests.
Hey, that's not a bad idea!

That night, Little Pea is too excited
to sleep. The idea of opening
a school is taking shape in his dreams...

When he wakes up, he's made up
his mind. He's going to open a school
for drawing. Hooray for Little Pea!

There! He has already put the sign up!
All that's left is to find students.

Soon, applicants begin lining up...

"Welcome! Have you been drawing for a long time?"
"No."

"What's your favorite color?"
"Yummy!"

"Do you like stamps?"
"What are stamps?!"

At the end of the day, Little Pea
has his first group of students.

The next day, classes begin.

The students are hard at work.
Some are quite good...

... while others are a bit less gifted.

And then there's... Tarantula.

Tarantula is very disciplined.
She always shows up on time every
morning. She's very friendly. But...

… her art is a disaster!

When asked to draw a butterfly…
She draws a pile of dots.

When asked to sketch a seashell…
It looks like a bunch of blue blots.

And an apple?
Everyone's seeing spots!

Tarantula's work is peculiar.
Maybe drawing isn't for her.
Perhaps Little Pea should tell her.

But it's not easy to shatter someone's
dream of becoming an artist...
What will Little Pea do?

Little Pea organizes a visit to the museum.
He has rented a van to get his students there.
There sure are a lot of people!

And so many exquisite
pieces to see!

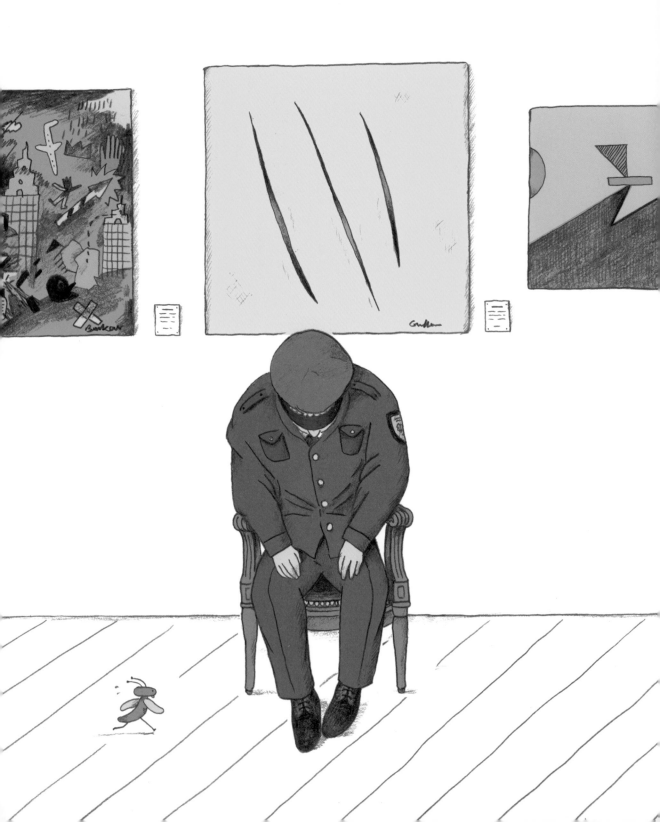

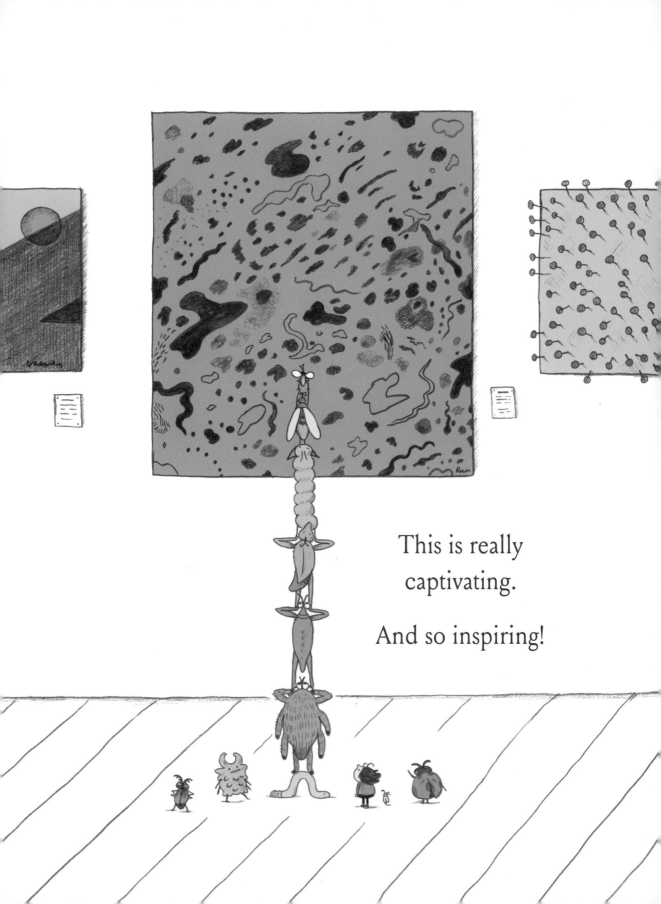

As the months pass, the students
prepare for the end-of-year show.
It's a portrait exhibition.
They've all made so much progress!

Little Pea comments on the work
of each student.

Let's see...   Hmm...

Good!   Interesting!

So original!

Very well executed!

And how should
we look at this?

It's now Tarantula's turn.
Let's see what she did...

"This is what you've been secretly working on! It's absolutely incredible!" Everyone is so impressed!

The first year at Little Pea's drawing school
has just ended — and all the students
have graduated! Hip hip hooray!

And who's been the semester's standout student?
None other than Tarantula!

This year, the students have learned to draw,
but their teacher, Little Pea, has also
learned a very important lesson:
One does not always recognize
a GREAT artist at first glance!